This Puffin book
belongs to

. . . .

. . . .

For Libby Allman and *In Other Words*, many thanks

PUFFIN BOOKS

Published by the Penguin Group
Penguin Books Ltd, 80 Strand, London WC2R ORL, England
Penguin Group (USA), Inc., 375 Hudson Street, New York, New York 10014, USA
Penguin Books Australia Ltd, 250 Camberwell Road, Camberwell, Victoria 3124, Australia
Penguin Books Canada Ltd, 10 Alcorn Avenue, Toronto, Ontario, Canada M4V 3B2
Penguin Books India (P) Ltd, 11 Community Centre, Panchsheel Park, New Delhi – 110 017, India
Penguin Group (NZ), cnr Airborne and Rosedale Roads, Albany, Auckland 1310, New Zealand
Penguin Books (South Africa) (Pty) Ltd, 24 Sturdee Avenue, Rosebank 2196, South Africa

Penguin Books Ltd, Registered Offices: 80 Strand, London WC2R ORL, England

puffinbooks.com

Published in 2004
7 9 10 8 6

Copyright © Tony Blundell, 2004

The moral right of the author/illustrator has been asserted

Set in PhoenixChunky 15/22pt

Manufactured in China

British Library Cataloguing in Publication Data
A CIP catalogue record for this book is available from the British Library

ISBN-13:978-0-67091-328-2 (Hardback)
ISBN-13:978-0-14056-917-9 (Paperback)

BEWARE
OF TEACHERS

Tony Blundell

PUFFIN

The wolf's larder was empty with not even a nettle or a slug to chew on. And as for a nice, plump boy or girl, he hadn't seen one for weeks. But as his tummy rumbled he started to think, where were all the children? At school, of course!

"That's where I'll find lots of children to gobble up!" he said.

So the wolf went to school.

All the children were lining up in the playground so the wolf trotted over and joined the end of the line.

The boys and girls eyed him warily, but the wolf put all thoughts of breakfast out of his mind and gave them his most angelic smile.

Just then, the bell rang and they all went inside.

When the teacher saw the wolf, she clapped her hands and smiled. "Why, I see we have a visitor joining us today," she said. "How very nice."

"But . . . Miss . . . Miss . . . MISS!" said the children.

"Miss, please Miss, he has a big bushy tail," said a boy.

"And very pointy ears!" said a girl. "And a big mouth full of very sharp . . ."

"That is quite enough, children," said the teacher. "I'm sure we will all do our best to make our visitor feel very welcome!" and she smiled again at the wolf. "Do take a seat, Mr . . . ?"

"Wolf," said the wolf.

"Well, what an interesting name – do take a seat and we will begin our lessons."

The wolf sat down obediently, but the chair was rather small and he had to tuck his tail through the hole in the back.

The children were already working hard. But how ever the wolf tried, his pencil didn't seem to work. No words or numbers came out of the end of it, just squiggles and scribble!

He looked around at the boys and girls and licked his lips – he was beginning to feel quite peckish!

After what seemed a very long time, a bell rang and all the children ran out into the playground.

"Aha!" said the wolf. "Dinner time!" and he raced off after them.

"Yummy, yummy, yummy, who's first in my tummy?" sang the wolf, and he chased the boys and girls around the playground.

But try as he might, the wolf couldn't catch any of them.

"Bother!" he panted as skipping ropes tangled around his arms and legs.

"Bother again!" he gasped as footballs rolled under his feet.

And "Oof!" he grunted as he finally went crashing to the ground.

When the wolf opened his eyes, he found himself surrounded by excited children.

"Right, Wolfy!" they said. "We know who you are, and we know that you want to gobble us all up!"

"Oh, not *all*," said the wolf, not wanting to appear greedy.

"Well, you won't be able to eat any of us like that, will you?" said the children.

"We could untie you, **Mr Wolf**, if you promise one thing . . . go and gobble up our teacher instead!" said a girl.
One teacher sounded better than no children, so the wolf agreed.

"She would make a much better meal than any of us," said a boy.

Very carefully, the children untied their skipping ropes and the rather confused wolf staggered off towards the classroom.

Just as he got there, the bell rang and the teacher called the children back inside. The wolf looked around for somewhere to hide.

"Aha," he thought, "I can hide in here and when the teacher opens the door . . ." He licked his lips. "Yummy, yummy, yummy, teacher in my tummy!"

He pulled open the door and leaped into the teacher's store cupboard.

It was very dark and the wolf's feet landed right in a box of marbles.

"Oooerr!" he said as his feet slid out from under him, and "Aaargh!" as he did a perfect somersault, and "Uuurgh!" as all the paint pots, glitter and glue showered down on top of him.

When the wolf opened his eyes, he found the teacher looking down at him, and she didn't look pleased!

"Well, really, Mr Wolf!" she said. "What a terrible mess! A store cupboard is really not the place for gymnastics. You are **NOT** a very clever wolf, are you?!"

The not-very-clever wolf looked up at the teacher's cross face and her waggy, pointy finger. He had suddenly lost his appetite.

"I do believe, **Mr Wolf**, that you were planning to leap out and gobble me up! But that wouldn't be very smart of you, would it? I am just a skinny teacher. Our headmaster is waiting outside for us, and he is big and fat and round! If you were clever, **Mr Wolf**, you would eat him up instead!"

The wolf, who was by now quite hypnotized by the teacher's wagging finger, meekly agreed.

When the children saw the bedraggled wolf emerge from the cupboard, they started to giggle.

"Children!" said the teacher sharply. "Where are our manners?"

"Mr Wolf has made himself a lovely costume," she said, giving the children a big wink. "He looks perfect to help us with our country dancing!"

And saying that, she lined the boys and girls up, with the rather puzzled wolf at the back, and they skipped out on to the field, where the headmaster was waiting for them. The wolf was starting to feel quite peckish again, and he was looking forward to meeting and eating a big, fat headmaster.

The headmaster beamed a big, welcoming smile.
"Good afternoon, boys and girls," he said. "I see we have a guest! You are very welcome, Mr . . . ?"
"Wolf!" said the wolf.
"And how clever of you to come dressed as King of the May!"

The wolf swelled with pride. He had never expected to become king just by going to school!

"And now," said the headmaster, with a little bow, "if your majesty would be so kind as to hold these ribbons above his head, we can begin our dance."

So the wolf took one end of the ribbons . . .

and the boys and girls grabbed the other . . .

and the music started to play.

Suddenly the wolf was surrounded by dancing children. His tummy was feeling very empty indeed.

The children danced round and round the hungry wolf, skipping in and out and around each other, the boys dancing one way, the girls the other.

And the more they danced, the closer they got to the wolf. He licked his lips. "Just a little closer," he thought, "and I can grab as many as I like . . . before moving on to the main course!"

Round and round danced the children . . .

round and round . . .

and rumble, rumble went the wolf's tummy . . .

until at last he could resist it no longer!

"Time for a bite to eat!" he said to himself, and he prepared to pounce.

It was at this moment that the wolf realized that he couldn't move at all! He was bound from head to toe in ribbons. All he could do was wrinkle his nose . . .

and wiggle his toes!

Before he could think what to do next, the music stopped and a bell rang somewhere in the school.

"Hooray! Home time!" shouted the children, and they raced away towards the school gates.

"**Well**, goodbye then, **Mr Wolf**," said the teacher. "Thank you so much for visiting us – it's been most entertaining! Do come again!" she said.

"**If** you're not too tied up!" added the headmaster, and they walked away across the field, laughing.

The wolf watched them go. "Bother!" he said.

Very much later, one bedraggled, bewildered, bad-tempered and very hungry wolf hopped miserably home in the moonlight.

"Grrr! If that is what school is all about," growled the wolf as he headed slowly back to his cave, "it's surprising those children learn anything at all."

But they do . . . don't they!